Industrial Conspiracies

Industrial Conspiracies

by Clarence Darrow

Mr. Darrow said:

I feel very grateful to you for the warmth and earnestness of your reception. It makes me feel sure that I am amongst friends. If I had to be tried again, I would not mind taking a change of venue to Portland (applause); although I think I can get along where I am without much difficulty.

The subject for tonight's talk was not chosen by me but was chosen for me. I don't know who chose it, nor just what they expected me to say, but there is not much in a name, and I suppose what I say tonight would be just about the same under any title that anybody saw fit to give.

I am told that I am going to talk about "Industrial Conspiracies." I ought to know something about them. And I won't tell you all I know tonight, but I will tell you some things that I know tonight.

The conspiracy laws, you know, are very old. As one prominent laboring man said on the witness stand down in Los Angeles a few weeks ago when they asked him if he was not under indictment and what for, he said he was under indictment for the charge they always made against working men when they hadn't done anything—conspiracy. And that is the charge they always make. It is the one they have always made against everybody when they wanted them, and particularly against working men, because they want them oftener than they do anybody else. (Applause).

When they want a working man for anything excepting work they want him for conspiracy. (Laughter). And the greatest conspiracy that is possible for a working man to be guilty of is not to work—a conspiracy the other fellows are always guilty of. (Applause). The conspiracy laws are very old. They were very much in favor in the Star Chamber days in England. If any king or ruler wanted to get rid of someone, and that someone had not done anything, they indicted him for what he was thinking about; that is, for conspiracy; and under it they could prove anything that he ever said or did, and anything that anybody else ever said or did to prove what he was thinking about; and therefore that he was guilty. And, of course, if anybody was thinking, it was a conspiracy against the king; for you can't think without thinking against a king. (Applause). The trouble is most people don't think. (Laughter and applause). And therefore they are not guilty of conspiracy. (Laughter and applause).

The conspiracy laws in England were especially used against working men, and in the early days, not much more than a hundred years ago, for one working man to go to another and suggest that he ask for higher wages was a conspiracy, punishable by imprisonment. For a few men to come together and form a labor organization in England was a conspiracy. It is not here. Even the employer is willing to let you form labor organizations, if you don't do anything but pass resolutions. (Laughter and applause).

But the formation of unions in the early days in England was a conspiracy, and so they used to meet in the forests and in the rocks and in the caves and waste places and hide their records in the earth where the informers and detectives and Burnes' men of those days could not get hold of them. (Applause). It used to be a crime for a working man to leave the county without the consent of the employer; and they never gave their consent. They were bought and sold with the land. Some of them are now. It reached that pass in England after labor unions were formed, that anything they did was a conspiracy, and to belong to one was practically a criminal offense. These laws were not made by Parliament; of course they were not made by the people. No law was ever made by the people; they are made for the people (applause); and it does not matter whether the people have a right to vote or not, they never make the laws. (Applause).

These laws, however, were made by judges, the same officials who make the laws in the United States today. (Applause).

We send men to the Legislature to make law, but they don't make them.

I don't care who makes a law, if you will let me interpret it. (Laughter). I would be willing to let the Steel Trust make a law if they would let me tell what it meant after they got it made. (Laughter). That has been the job of the judges, and that is the reason the powerful interests of the world always want the courts. They let you have the members of the Legislature, and the Aldermen and the Constable, if they can have the judges.

And so in England the judges by their decisions tied the working man hand and foot until he was a criminal if he did anything but work, as many people think he is today. He actually was at that time, until finally Parliament, through the revolution of the people, repealed all these laws that judges had made, wiped them all out of existence, and did, for a time at least, leave the working man free; and then they began to organize, and it has gone on to that extent in England today, that labor organizations are as firmly established as Parliament itself. Much better established there than here.

We in this country got our early laws from England. We took pretty much everything that was bad from England and left most that was good. (Applause). At first, when labor organizations were started they had a fair chance; they were left comparatively free; but when they began to grow the American judges got busy. They got busy with injunctions, with conspiracy laws, and there was scarcely anything that a labor organization could do that was not an industrial conspiracy.

Congress took a hand, not against labor; but to illustrate what I said about the difference between making a law and telling what the law means, we might refer to the act which was considered a great law at the time of its passage, a law defining conspiracy and combinations in reference to trade, the Sherman anti-trust law. In the meantime, the combinations of capital had grown so large that even respectable people began to be afraid of them, farmers and others who never learn anything until everybody else has forgotten it (laughter); they began to be afraid of them. They found the great industrial organizations of the country controlling everything they used. One powerful organization owned all the oil there was in the United States; another handful of men owned all the anthracite coal there was in the United States; a few men owned all the iron mines in the United States; and the people began to be alarmed about it. And so they passed a law punishing conspiracies against trade. The father of the law was Senator Sherman of Ohio. The law was debated long in Congress and the Senate. Every man spoke of it as a law against the trusts and monopolies, conspiracies in restraint of trade and commerce. Every newspaper in the country discussed it as that; every labor organization so considered it.

Congress passed it and the President signed it, and then an indictment was found against a corporation, and it went to the Supreme Court of the United States for the Supreme Court to say what the law meant. Of course Congress can't pass a law that you and I can understand. (Laughter). They may use words that are only found in the primer, but we don't know what they mean. Nobody but the Supreme Court can tell what they mean.

Everybody supposed this law was plain and simple and easily understood, but when they indicted a combination of capital for a conspiracy in restraint of trade, the Supreme Court said this law did not apply to them at all; that it was never meant to fit that particular case. So they tried another one, and they indicted another combination engaged in the business of cornering markets, engaged in the business of trade, rich people, good people. It means the same thing. (Laughter). And the Supreme Court decided that this law did not fit their case, and every one began to wonder what the law did mean anyhow. And after awhile there came along the strike of a body of laboring men, the American Railway Union. They didn't have a dollar in the world altogether, because they were laboring men and they were not engaged in trade; they were working; but they hadn't found anything else that the Sherman anti-trust act applied to, so they indicted Debs and his followers for a conspiracy in restraint of trade; and they carried this case to the Supreme Court. I was one of the attorneys who carried it to the Supreme Court. Most lawyers only tell you about the cases they win. I can tell you about some I lose. (Applause). A lawyer who wins all his cases does not have many. (Laughter).

Debs was indicted for a conspiracy in restraint of trade. It is not quite fair to say that I lost that case, because he was indicted and fearing he might get out on the indictment the judge issued an injunction against him. (Laughter). The facts were the same as if a man were suspected of killing somebody and a judge would issue an injunction against him for shooting his neighbor and he would kill his neighbor with a pistol shot and then they would send him to jail for injuring his clothes for violating an injunction. (Laughter). Well, they indicted him and they issued an injunction against him for the same thing. Of course, we tried the indictment before a jury, and that we won. You can generally trust a part of a jury anyhow, and very often all of them. But the court passed on the injunction case, and while the facts were just the same and the law was just the same, the jury found him innocent, but the court found him guilty. (Laughter). And Judge Wood said that he had violated the injunction. Then we carried it to the Supreme Court on the ground that the Sherman anti-trust law, which was a law to punish conspiracies in restraint of trade, was not meant for labor unions but it was meant for people who are trading, just as an ordinary common man would understand the meaning of language, but the Supreme Court said we didn't know anything about the meaning of language and that they had at last found what the Sherman anti-trust law meant and that it was to break up labor unions; and they sent Mr. Debs to jail under that law (laughter and applause), and nobody, excepting someone connected with the union had ever been sent to jail under that law, and probably never will be.

So of course, even the employer, the Merchants' and Manufacturers' Association and the Steel Trust, even they would be willing to let the Socialists go to the Legislature and make the laws, as long as they can get the judges to tell what the law means. (Loud applause). For the courts are the bulwarks of property, property rights and property interests, and they always have been. I don't know whether they always will be. I suppose they will always be, because before a man can be elected a judge he must be a lawyer.

They did patch up the laws against combinations in restraint of trade. Even the fellows who interpreted it, were ashamed of it and they fixed it up so they might catch somebody else, and they brought a case against the Tobacco Trust, and after long argument and years of delay the Supreme Court decided on the Tobacco Trust and they decided that this was a combination in restraint of trade, but they didn't send anybody to jail. They didn't even fine them. They gave them six months—not in jail, but six months in which to remodel their business so it would conform to the law, which they did. (Applause and laughter). But plug tobacco is selling just as high as it ever was, and higher.

They brought an action against the Standard Oil Trust—Mr. Roosevelt's enemy. (Laughter and applause). That is what he says. (Laughter and applause). They brought an action against the Standard Oil Trust to dissolve the Trust and they listened patiently for a few years—the Supreme Court is made up of old men, and they have got lots of time (laughter)—and after a few years they found out what the people had known for twenty-five years, that it was a trust, and they so decided that this great corporation had been a conspiracy in restraint of trade for years, had been fleecing the American people. I don't suppose anybody would have brought an action against them, excepting that they had a corner on gasoline and the rich people didn't like to pay so much for gasoline to run their automobiles. (Laughter and applause). They found out that the Standard Oil Company was guilty of a conspiracy under the Sherman anti-trust law, and they gave them six months in which to change the form of their business, and Standard Oil stock today is worth more than it ever was before in the history of the world, and gasoline has not been reduced in price, nor anything else that they have to sell. There never has been an instance since that law was passed where it has ever had the slightest effect upon any combination of capital, but under it working men are promptly sent to jail; and it was passed to protect the working man and the consumer against the trusts of the United States. So, you see, it does not make much difference what kind of a law we make as long as the judges tell us what it means.

The Steel Trust has not been hurt. They are allowed to go their way, and they have taken property, which at the most, is worth three hundred million dollars and have capitalized it and bonded it for a billion and a half, or five dollars for every one that it represents, and the interests and dividends which have been promptly paid year by year have come from the toil and the sweat and the life of the American workingman. (Applause). And nobody interferes with the Steel Trust; at least, nobody but the direct action men. (Laughter and applause). The courts are silent, the states' attorneys are silent; the governors are silent; all the officers of the law are silent, while a great monster combination of crooks and criminals are riding rough-shod over the American people. (Applause). But it is the working man who is guilty of the industrial conspiracy. They and their friends are the ones who are sent to jail. It is the powerful and the strong who have the keys to the jails and the penitentiaries, and there is not much danger of their locking themselves in jails and penitentiaries. The working man never did have the keys. Their business has been to build them and to fill them.

There have been other industrial conspiracies, however, which are the ones that interest me most, and it is about these and what you can do about them and what you can't do about them that I wish to talk tonight.

The real industrial conspiracies are by the other fellow. It is strange that the people who have no property have been guilty of all of the industrial conspiracies, and the people who own all the earth have not been guilty of any industrial conspiracy. It is like our criminal law. Nearly all the laws are made to protect property; nearly all the crimes are crimes against property, and yet only the poor go to jail. That is, all the people in our jail have committed crimes against property, and yet they have not got a cent. The people outside have so much property they don't know what to do with it, and they have committed no crime against property. So with the industrial conspiracies, those who are not in trade or commerce are the ones who have been guilty of a conspiracy to restrict trade and commerce, and those who are in trade and commerce that have all the money have not been guilty of anything. Their business is prosecuting other people so they can keep what they have got and get what little there is left.

But there are real industrial conspiracies. They began long ages ago, and they began by direct action, when the first capitalist took his club and knocked the brains out of somebody who wanted a part of it for himself. That is direct action. They got the land by direct action. They went out and took it. If anybody was there, they drove them off or killed them, as the case might be. It is only the other fellow that can't have direct action. They got all their title to the earth by direct action. Of course, they have swapped it more or less, since, but the origin is there. They just went out and took possession of it, and it is theirs. And the strong have always done it; they have reached out and taken possession of the earth.

A few men today can control all the industry and do control all of the industry of this country. A dozen men sitting around the table in a big city can bring famine if they wish; they can paralyze the wheels of industry from one end of the United States to the other, and the prosperity of villages, cities and towns, and the wages of its people depends almost entirely upon the wills of a dozen men.

They have taken the mines; and all the coal there is in the United States, or practically all, is controlled today by a few railroad companies who can tell us just what we must pay, and if we are not willing to pay it, we can freeze; and we respect private property so much that we will stand around and freeze rather than take the coal that nature placed in the earth for all mankind. (Applause).

All the iron ore in the United States that is worth taking is owned and controlled by the Steel Trust, one combination with a very few men managing the business; not more than a half a dozen absolutely controlling it have their will; and nobody can have any iron ore, or mold it or use it, excepting at the will of a few men who have taken possession of what nature placed there for all of us, if we were wise enough to use it and understand it. And the great forests of the United States, what is left of them—and there is not so very much left. We are a wise people. We pass laws now for the protection of timber in the United States, so it won't be destroyed too fast, and at the same time, we put a tariff duty of two dollars a thousand on lumber that comes from somewhere else so that it will be destroyed at a high price. (Laughter and applause). We are the wisest set of people of any land that the sun ever shone upon. And if you don't believe it, ask Roosevelt when he comes here. (Laughter and applause).

A few men control what is left of the forests, a few men and a few great corporations have taken the earth, what is good of it. They have left the arid lands, the desert and the mountains which nobody can use,—the desert for sand heaps and the mountains for scenery. They are now taxing the people to build reservoirs so that the desert will blossom; and after it begins to blossom, they will take that. (Applause). And even if they didn't own the land, they own all the ways there are of getting to it, and they are able to take from the farmer just so much of his grain as they see fit to take, and so far as the farmer is concerned, I wish they would take it all (laughter and applause), because he always has been against the interests of every man that toils, including himself. (Applause). And they are able to say to the working man engaged in industry just how much of his product they will take, and from him they take just enough to leave him alive. They have got to leave him alive, or he can't work, and they have got to leave him enough strength and ambition to propagate his species or the rich people can't get their work done in the next generation. And that is all that they are bound to leave him.

They own the railroads, the mills, the factories, and all the tools and implements of trade and commerce, and the workingman has only one thing to sell. That is his labor, his life; and he has to sell that to the highest bidder.

There are only a few of these men who own the earth and all of its fullness. There are millions and millions of the people who do the work, and if you can keep these millions and millions disorganized and competing with each other, they will keep wages down themselves without any help from the bosses. (Loud applause). On the other hand, there are so few men who own the earth and the tools that they find it perfectly easy to combine with each other and regulate the price of their products, and they have learned better than to compete, and there is no way for the wit of man to make and interpret any law which will ever set them to competing again. They have managed to control the price of their products, and charge what they see fit and all they need is to buy their raw material in the open markets of the world as cheaply as they can, and labor is the principal raw material that they use. So of course they want free trade in labor, and protection in commodities; and they have always had it, and our wise Americans that are the marvel of the day, including the working people, have cheerfully given them protection in the commodities that they sell and free trade in the labor which they buy. (Applause). And they thought by protecting the Steel Trust, so there can't be any foreign competition that it will make the Steel Trust so rich that they can afford to pay high prices to their working men. It is one thing to make a man rich enough so he can afford to pay high wages; it is another thing to make him pay. (Laughter).

So the employer and the capitalist have combined in all industry, and they fix the price to suit themselves and insist that the workingman shall come to them individually and unorganized and compete with each other for a day's labor, so they can buy labor at the smallest cost and if, perchance, there are not working men enough here, they want the ports of the world opened so they can draw on China or Japan or any other country on the face of the earth, and get working men there to work for them at the smallest price.

The game is simple and easy. It seems as if it were simple enough for an American farmer to understand; but he doesn't. (Laughter).

Now, the original conspiracy, industrial conspiracy, has been on the part of the strong to take the earth, and they have got it. They own it, and all they need now is to get enough working men and women at a low enough price to make them as much wealth as they want. It is pretty hard to fill that market, they want so much; but that is all they need. And the conspiracy on the other side of the workingman of the United States is the same conspiracy as the conspiracy of the workingman of the world, and it has only one object. We may temporize; we may be content with a little; we may stop at half measures, but in the end it only has one object, and that is for the workers of the world to take back the earth that has been taken from us. (Cries of hurrah and loud cheering).

Take it back, and have all the products of their toil, not part of it, but all of it. Now, it is a long road. It is a universal, world-wide conspiracy by the intelligent working people and by their friends the world over to get back the earth that has been stolen by direct action. (Applause).

Now, no one who understands this question wants anything less and the employer is right when he says if workingmen are permitted to organize they won't stop with that; and they won't. (Applause). You may place every lawyer on the bench and you may place a jail in every block and a penitentiary in every ward, and the workingmen won't stop. (Applause). If they will, they deserve to be workingmen forever. (Applause).

The employer understands that if workingmen organize something will be doing; and so he does not believe in organization. Sometimes he says he does, but he does not. If workingmen must organize, then the thing is to keep them as quiet as they can, to turn their labor meetings into prayer meetings. (Laughter and applause). They are entirely harmless. They don't help the people who pray, and the Lord has always been so far away from the workingman that it doesn't bother Him either. (Laughter). They are willing even, as I have said, to let them pass resolutions, but that is about the limit. (Laughter). They understand that one thing leads to another, and if they concede higher wages today, next year they will want another raise and so they will. There is no danger of raising it too high for a long while to come. And if they concede shorter hours today, next year they may want them shorter still. Everybody is working for shorter hours, especially the people who don't work. And they are all working for bigger pay; even those who get all there is, they want more. And of course, there will be no stopping, there will be no end to the demand, until we get it all, and that is a long way off.

And the question is how? And that is not so easy. It is easier to tell how you can't get it than to tell how you can get it. It is easier to tell how you haven't got it than how you are going to get it.

There is another thing that they are fairly well satisfied with: They don't worry much about voting. They have been satisfied to let all the men vote, and they have still kept their property. (Laughter). They will be satisfied to let all the women vote, and they will still keep their property. Voting has not done very much. We have been practicing at it for more than a hundred years, and it is a nice little toy to keep people satisfied, but that is all it has done so far. (Applause).

Of course, here and there we have been able to pass a few laws. For instance, we have statutes which forbid women from working in a factory more than ten hours a day. (Laughter). Now, we have done something. (Laughter and applause). We have statutes forbidding men to labor more than a certain number of hours a day. That is, people like to work; they love it so dearly that you have to pass a law to keep a working man from working. (Laughter).

When we pass laws to keep men and women from working it ought to show the stupidest mind that there is something terribly wrong with the industrial conditions under which we live. If men had a chance to work and get all the proceeds of their work, you would not have to pass laws to keep them from working. They would stop soon enough. And if every man could employ his own labor and receive the full product of his toil it would make no difference how hard your neighbor worked, it would not hurt you in the least, and you could let him work himself to death if he wanted to.

The only difficulty is under the patch work industrial system of today where a few men own all the earth, and all the factories and mills and are compelled to sell their product to the workingman, they give him such a small share of that product that the workingmen haven't anything to buy it with. They can't buy it back, and so there is not work enough to go around. And for that reason we are tinkering up this old system of laws to keep people from working, and we pass a law to limit the number of hours that a man can work and to limit the number of hours that a woman can work, and to limit the age at which a little child can be fed into a factory or a mill.

Do you suppose that the fatherhood and the motherhood of the people of the United States is not of a high enough grade so they would not send their children to a factory or a mill if there was any way to avoid it? And do you think under any fair system of industry and life we would ever need a law to keep a child out of a factory or a mill? (Applause).

We have managed to pass some laws to require safety appliances in factories and in mills and upon railroads. For instance, to put a guard on a buzz saw so that a workingman won't saw his hand instead of sawing the wood. (Laughter). But if a workingman had any chance to employ his labor and get what he produced he would not be fooling with a buzz saw and there would be no need of it and he would look out for the safety of the machines himself and do it a great deal better than the Government ever did it or can ever possibly do it. (Applause). So we have done everything and tried everything, excepting to strike at the root of any evil and accomplish something of real value. We have even passed laws excluding the Chinaman and the Jap from the United States. That is, we love our own people so dearly that we won't let the Chinaman or the Jap do the work for them. (Laughter). We want our people to have all the work, and if they come here and volunteer to do it we won't let them; for work is a blessing under the present industrial system. We have to work. If we stop we starve.

Now, I could imagine a system, and it seems to me that most all of you could imagine a system that was so fair and so just and so equal that if any body of philanthropic heathens would agree to come over here and do our work for us, we would go and play golf or run automobiles whilst they were doing it; but with a condition of life where a few men have it all and the rest can only live if they have the work to do, why no one can do it for us; we have got to do it ourselves. We can't even allow a machine to do it, for every time we get the machine to do the work it takes the place of a man or two, or more, and they go out to beg or tramp or starve, as the case may be.

We have got a wonderful system of industry, and industrial life. If anybody ever invented it, which they didn't, he must have been standing on his head and drunken at the time he did it. (Laughter and applause).

And now what are we going to do about it? We have the great mass of men living upon the will of a few and taking what they can get, and we have got to get back the earth. A small job. Some people would say, "Well, if you have got to get it back why don't you go and take it?" Well, we don't. Some people say we have got to vote it back, and some say we have got to get it back through labor organizations, and some say we have got to have a good deal more than that.

I don't know. But I want to say some things about political action. If we are going to get at it in that way we first had better understand the size of the contract, and there are a great many people who don't. (Applause).

We have been voting a long time, and we have a democracy. Everybody can vote—every man past twenty-one. If we are not doing well enough we are going to let the women vote; then if we don't do any better we will let the children vote, and then we will get somewhere. (Applause). If we are going to get out of this muss by voting, why, let's have a little of it. We had better have an election every day, because if we can do it that way it is about the simplest there is. But we have been working at it a long while and we are getting in worse all the time.

In the first place, how many of us understand our system of government? We hear people talk about it on the Fourth day of July, and they run for an office in the fall. The most glorious system ever invented by the wit of man!

I want to say that it is about the craziest system that was ever conceived in the brain of man. (Applause).

Our system of government never was conceived in the brain of man, because no man or combination of men were ever foolish enough and weak enough to conceive them. It is a system of blunders. If you would elect for the next hundred years a president as wise as Roosevelt (laughter and applause) you could not move a peg.

Let me just tell you why. Suppose we want to pass a law. As I have said, we pass little fool laws and nobody pays much attention to them. They don't hurt anybody and they let them go. But suppose we want to pass a law of substance, if there is any such thing as a law of substance; suppose we want to do it, something affecting fundamental rights, now how are we going to get at it?

One hundred and twenty-five years ago and more a body of men, very wise for their day and generation, met to form the constitution. They had just been indulging in a little direct action against England. (Laughter). They could have sent members to Parliament up to now and we would have still been British subjects. I don't know as we would have been any worse off if we had been. But they got at it simply and directly, and so they won our American independence. I don't know just when it was lost, but they won it. (Applause). And the first thing they did was to have a constitution.

You can't do anything without a constitution. You have got to have a good constitution to get anywhere.

And so they got together a body of men, John Hancock and some more penmen, and they wrote a constitution.

Now, what is a constitution? Why, it is just the same as if a boy, twenty-one years of age, would say, "Well, now, I have become of age, and I am wise, and I am going to write out a constitution to cover the rest of my life, and when I am forty I can't do anything that is unconstitutional."

There wasn't a railroad one hundred and twenty-five years ago; there wasn't a steam engine; there wasn't a flying machine, of course, nor an automobile. Nobody knew anything about electricity, except what came down from the clouds and they were busy dodging it. There were few machines; there was just a body of farmers—that's all. (Laughter and applause). And they wrote the constitution, and there it is. It didn't apply to the industrial conditions of today, for they didn't know anything about the industrial conditions of today, but they imagined that they were so wise that lest people one hundred and twenty-five years later should think they knew more they would tie things up so that we could not make a fool of ourselves, to the third or fourth generation after they were dead. (Laughter). And so they wrote down a constitution which meant that whatever the American people wanted to do a hundred, or two hundred, or five hundred years afterward, they could not do it unless it agreed with the constitution that had already been written down or unless they changed it.

Well now, that was a wise piece of business so far, wasn't it? But that is only the beginning of it.

Then they organized this government into separate states. I don't know how many there are now, they are hatching some new ones all the while. But every state was independent in a way, and in a way it was united with all the rest. Nobody knows just how much independence there is and how much union there is. Nobody knows but the judges, and they only know in the particular case. They can say this goes or this does not go; nobody can tell until they get there. (Laughter). What comes within the state province and what comes within the national province nobody knows, nor ever did know. The states are individual and separate to make laws for themselves. Each one of them has a law factory of their own, and they are all busy; and the United States Government has another big law factory, and they have all been grinding out laws for a hundred years and not only that but the courts have been telling us what they mean and what they don't mean; so it has been pretty busy for the lawyer.

Then they decided that they should have a congress, which consisted of the senate, where men were selected for six years, not by the people but by state legislatures, and a congress where men were elected for two years by the people. But these congressmen elected for two years didn't take their seat for a year after they were elected, and time to forget all about the issue on which they were elected. (Laughter). And not satisfied with that, they had to have a Supreme Court to tell us what congress or the senate meant, and the Supreme Court was appointed for life and not beholden to anybody; and they are generally about a hundred years old apiece. (Laughter). And then they had a president, who was elected for four years, and who had a right to veto anything that congress and the senate saw fit to pass, and if he vetoed it you could not pass it except by a two-thirds majority of both houses. And there you have got it, so far as the United States Government is concerned. But that is not nearly all.

So if you want to pass some important law, let's see what you have to do. Of course, little laws don't count, for you can't keep up a factory unless you do something, pass laws one year and repeal them the next, or some little thing like that, to save the job. But take an important thing, an issue coming up from the people, one ultimately meaning the taking of the earth. Nothing else is important. It may be in one form or another, but it must have that purpose, or it won't be important, because you can't regulate things that belong to other people very successfully; you have got to get it yourselves. (Applause). Now, let's see what you have got to do.

In the first place, you must elect a congress, and the congress does not take its seat for a year after they are elected; and then they run up against the United States senate, holding six year terms, and one-third of them passing away each two years, none of them elected upon the issue upon which congress were elected, mostly old men and generally rich men—rich enough to get the job. (Laughter). Now you have got to get the law through congress and through the senate both, which is well nigh impossible, if it is a law of any consequence. And then here comes a president, who is elected by the people for four years, and he must sign it, and if congress and the senate or the president refuses, then you can't do it. Excepting if the president refuses then you have got to get two-thirds of both the houses, which is impossible if the law amounts to anything, and then you have only begun. If you should happen to get all these three at once, which we never did and never will on anything very important because the claws are all cut out of any bill before it ever gets very far,—then you have only begun. Then here is this document, this sacred document which came down from Mount Sinai one hundred and twenty-five years ago, The Constitution, and you lay down the law beside the Constitution and see whether it is unconstitutional or not and of course you could not tell. You would not know anything about it. Congress could not tell; the senate could not tell; the president could not tell. There is only one tribunal that could tell, and that is the Supreme Court. And while the Constitution fills about ten pages, the interpretation of the Constitution will fill a hundred volumes or more. (Laughter). And the Constitution is not what is written in ten pages but it is what is written in the decisions of the judges covering over a hundred years; and they don't always agree, at that, which makes some of them right. If they all agreed probably none of them would be right. (Laughter).

So if you should ever succeed in getting a law past congress with its two year term, and the senate with its six, and the president with his four, any one of whom may block it, and will, if it is important, then you have got to pass it to these wise judges who are not elected at all and who have no interests with the people because they are holding their office for life and they have been there so long and got so old that they don't understand any of the new questions anyhow, and could not, and who have the conservatism of age anyway, and they have got to decide whether that law is constitutional or not, and before they have decided it and before it has run the gauntlet of all of them, even if they decided it right you would not need the law. The law would be dead. (Laughter). But you must combine on all these four things before you can accomplish anything.

And that is not all. Then you must decide whether the law is within the province of the state or the nation; whether it is state business or whether it is national business; and most of our laws are state laws and when we get back to the state we find the same old story. Wonderful wisdom! Here is first a constitution, which is nothing except as I illustrated, a boy twenty-one years old swears he won't know any more when he is fifty, and that kind of a boy generally does not. (Laughter). And we have a legislative body to make laws, composed of a house and a senate, two bodies, one not being wise enough to make them themselves; and we have a governor with a veto, and a Supreme Court to say whether the law is constitutional or not. The same thing in the state and the same thing in the nation. Then we have got to see whether it is in the province of the nation or the state, and you see it is next to impossible to ever get a constitutional law that amounts to anything, and we have never done it.

But, they say, this is a country where people vote, and if you don't like the law, why change it. If you didn't vote there would be some excuse for direct action, but as long as you vote you can change the law. (Applause). The trouble is you can't change it. You haven't got a chance. How can you change one of these laws that are important? How can you appeal to the people, first of all, and change it with the people? And next, how could you possibly elect a congress and a senate and a president and a Supreme Court all at once, that ever would make any substantial change, or ever did?

"Well," they say, "if the Constitution fetters you too much, why, change the Constitution. The Constitution provides that it can be changed." And so it does; but how?

You can change the Constitution of the United States. You could change Mt. Hood, but it would take a pile of shovels. (Laughter). You could change Mt. Hood a good deal easier. It could be done. The law provides that if you pass a law through congress and the senate and it is signed by the president, to change the Constitution, you may submit it to the people and if three-fourths of all the states in the Union consent to it, why you can change it. What do you think of that?

Do you suppose there is any power on earth that ever could get a law through congress and the senate, approved by the senate, and then get three-fourths of the individual states in the Union to approve it? You and your children and your children's children would die while you are doing it.

The best proof of that is the fact that we have had a constitution for one hundred and twenty-five years, and the Lord knows it needs patching. It needs something worse: It needs abolishing worse than anything else. (Applause).

If anybody does want to tinker with voting the first thing necessary is to get rid of the constitution. We have had one for a hundred and twenty-five years with a provision for changing it. It has needed change. It needs it all the while, and yet it has never been changed but once. They passed several amendments all in a heap. What were those? Those were amendments growing out of the Civil War, and they didn't permit any of the Southern States to vote. They just ran them over their heads, and they were all amendments protecting the negroes after enfranchisement. And those are the only amendments we have had in one hundred and twenty-five years, and it took a war to get those—considerable direct action.

Why, if a body of ingenious men had gotten together to make the frame work of a government to absolutely take from the people all the power they possibly could, they could not have contrived anything more mischievous and complete than our American form of government. (Applause).

Russia is easy and simple compared with this. If you did happen to get a progressive, kindly, sympathetic, humane Czar, which you probably won't, but if you did you could change all the laws of Russia and you could change them right away and get something. But if you got the wisest and kindest and most sympathetic man on earth at the head of our government he could not do anything; or if you filled congress with them they could not do anything, or the senate they could not, and the Supreme Court could not. You would have to fill them all at once, and then they would have to override all the precedents of a hundred and twenty-five years to accomplish it.

The English Government is simplicity itself compared to it. As compared with ours it is as direct as a convention of the I. W. W. (Applause). The English people elect a Parliament and when some demand comes up from the country for different legislation which reaches Parliament and is strong enough to demand a division in Parliament and the old majority fails, Parliament is dissolved at once, and you go right straight back to the people and elect a new Parliament upon that issue and they go at once to Parliament and pass a law, and there is no power on earth that can stop them. The king hasn't any more to say about the laws of England, nor any more power than a floor manager of a charity ball would have to say about it. He is just an ornament, and not much of an ornament at that. (Applause). The House of Lords is comparatively helpless, and they never had any constitution; there never was any power in England to set aside any law that the people made. It was the law, plain and direct and simple, and you might get somewhere with it. But we have built up a machine that destroys every person who undertakes to touch it. I don't know how you are ever going to remedy it. Nothing short of a political revolution, which would be about as complete as the Deluge, could ever change our laws under our present system (applause) in any important particular.

But while anybody is voting they had better vote the right way if they can find it out. If they can't it is just as well not to vote. They had better vote for some workingman's candidate and be counted as long as you are doing it. (Applause). Still any benefit that must come anywhere in the near future must come some other way. Workingmen have not raised their wages by it; they haven't shortened their hours of toil by it; they haven't improved the conditions of life by it; it has all been done in some other way. All of this has been accomplished by trades-unionism, by organization. If you can organize workingmen sufficiently so that they may make their demands strong enough you can accomplish something in all of these directions. (Applause). But our political institutions are such that before you could get anything like a political revolution you need an industrial revolution. (Applause).

And then we come to face some of the problems of today, and I want to speak a little bit about that. I have talked to you about as long as I ought to tonight, but I want to say something about some matters that perhaps are closer home than those.

We find the American workingman bound by the law, as I have said,—everything taken from him. He can't do anything by voting. The courts are almost always against him, for the simple reason that courts are made from lawyers, generally prominent lawyers and well known lawyers. In almost every instance these lawyers have been corporation lawyers. Their instincts are that way. Their beliefs are that way, and their training and heredity are that way; and they are not with the poor.

In order to be a lawyer you must spend considerable time, if not studying, at least you must spend it not working. You can't work while you are becoming a lawyer, and you won't work afterwards. (Laughter). It takes eight or ten years' schooling at least. That is one reason why a lawyer says he should have big fees, it takes him so long to learn the trade. That is, the poor people support a lawyer so long while he is preparing that they ought to support him better while he is practicing (laughter); because a fellow studying to be a lawyer, or a doctor, or a minister—I don't know what they study to be a minister, but I suppose they do (laughter)—has got to be living while he is studying and somebody must take care of him; to take care of him while he is learning—after he gets it learned he takes care of himself.

So the judges are not on your side. They don't look at things the way you do. They are trained differently. If they were picked out of your trade councils they would look at them differently and they could decide cases differently. Everything is in habit, and the environment and the training, and they are all the time fashioning the law against you.

Then what? Workingmen find themselves hedged about wherever they turn. They can't employ themselves. Somebody has got the earth. They can't mine ore; somebody owns it. They can't get the steel to do the work with themselves; they have got to buy it off somebody. They can't do the work except for wages; the employer does it and the employer insists upon open competition in labor and workingmen are constantly fighting each other.

Everybody admits that the systems must change, that the laws must change. They can't change them by political action, and the injustice goes on, and on, and on.

They find children taken from school and put in factories and mills; their children, not the children of the rich but the children of the poor. The rich love their children so much that they don't put them in factories and mills. Only the children of the poor are put in factories and mills, which shows that mother love is not the same with poor people as it is with rich people. Still the poor people have all the children anyway, so there are enough. (Laughter). They are good to the rich and they have the children for them.

They find that the life of a poor man is only about two-thirds as long as that of a rich man. A man dies because he is poor. A lawyer, or preacher or a doctor can take care of himself; but the workingman dies because he is poor. Lots of gray-headed lawyers and preachers and bankers and doctors, but there are not so very many gray-haired workingmen. That is lucky for them, too, because they would have to go to the poor house. (Laughter). Maybe they will get old age pensions sometimes. (Applause). It is always safe and economical to give workingmen old age pensions, because they never reach old age. They find themselves ground up by all kinds of machinery, ground to death under car wheels, sawed to pieces in factories and mills, falling from ten and twelve story buildings, picked up on the ground just one big spatter of blood and bones. They know these conditions are wrong and they can't change them, and the people who have control of it are squeezing them tighter and tighter all the time and they don't know which way to turn. And which way do they turn? They try voting. They don't accomplish it. They try organization, and that is hard. They try direct action, and that is hard, too. You wonder that they try it.

Now, a great many people condemned the McNamaras. A great many working people condemned them. I don't say that the working people ever need to resort to force, or ever should resort to force, but it is not for me to condemn anybody who believes they should. (Applause).

I know that the progress of the human race is one long bloody story of force and violence (applause); and from the time man got up on his hind legs and looked the world in the face he has been fighting, and fighting, and fighting for all the liberty and the opportunity that he has had. I think the time will come when he can stop. Perhaps it has come. And no one hates cruelty and force and violence more than I hate it. But don't let them ever tell you that all the force has been on our side. (Loud applause). It never has been; most all of it has been with them. (Applause). They are the ones who have the force, who have the power.

Why are these standing armies and navies; and, more than that, the militia building their armories in every great city in the United States? Are they there for a foreign foe or are they there to shoot strikers and workingmen when the time shall come? (Loud applause). Are they there to protect the people from China and Japan and England, or are they there to protect property against the poor? (Loud and prolonged applause).

What is a lockout in a factory or mill when they call it famine and want and hunger and cold, to do their work? Is that force, or is it peace and quietness and gentleness, and the Golden Rule?

What are the policemen, what are the officers of the law, what is the machinery of government directed against the workingmen, holding all the resources of the earth in the power of a few and compelling the money to go to those few for the means of life? Isn't this force?

What is the blacklist? Is it anything but force that drives children into the factories, that drives women into factories, and compels men to work with defective machinery for long hours and poor wages? Is it anything but the force of starvation and want that has always been used by the owners of the earth to make the poor do their bidding and their will?

The force is there. It is not with the weak. The weak have never had the strength or the opportunity to use the force. And when here and there some man like the McNamaras and others—I don't need to mention them alone, excepting that I want to live to see the day that justice will be done to them (loud applause)—here and there when they reach out blindly to meet force with force, call it blind if you will, call it wrong if you will; I have never counseled it or advised it, perhaps because I am not brave enough; it is not for me to say; but call it blind, call it mistaken, call it what you will; but the fact will ever remain that men who do it never do it for their own mean personal ends but because they love their fellowmen. (Loud applause). And long ago it was written down that "Greater love hath no man than this, that he who would give his life for his friend." Some day, I say, it will be understood, and some day the world will understand that they and Wood who was indicted from the other side for an attempt to charge something to labor that labor was not guilty of, and all of these other indictments growing out of the same acts, that all of these acts were not individual acts at all, but they were a part of a great industrial tragedy of a great evolution of society; that they are what are called social crimes or social acts for which these men were responsible in no degree. They were a part of a machine; they were risking their lives; a part of a system; and, do what you will, others will be ground out of it forever and forever, until the system shall change and until there will be some equity and justice in the world. (Loud applause).

The world is changing, and every person is doing his part in his own way. It is not for you to criticize me or for me to criticize you, but to judge men by their motives and to judge them by the side they are on. Labor must stand for its own men. (Loud applause). It must stand even for its own mistakes, and its own crimes if it is guilty of them. (Applause). There is one question, and only one, to ask concerning a man or concerning an act: "Was he on my side?" (Applause). You may counsel him to do differently; yes. You may teach him moderation, and believe in it; and all of us want to see peace and justice and harmony come out of all of these contending forces, as it one day will come; you may teach it and you may believe it, but the man who lets a thought loose in the universe can never tell what the results of that thought may be. It may bear fruit in a thousand ways of which we never dream; but even though it does and it must the thought must go forth to do its work and to change the face of the earth. The highest and the holiest and the best thought may bring on strife and war. And John Brown, a devoted man who believed in the liberty of the slaves, took his gun in his hand and went to Virginia and raised his hand in rebellion against the country. He was tried and convicted and hanged for murder, and he was guilty of murder under the laws of man, but under the laws of God he was a hero. The laws of justice and righteousness look not to the act but they look at the motive that moved the brain. Were they fighting on our side? Were they fighting for justice and humanity and the weak and the poor and the oppressed, as they saw it? If so, whoever they are and whatever, they demand our sympathy and our support. (Applause).

John Brown by his act of heroism plunged the United States into a civil war costing hundreds of thousands of lives, and billions of property. But he was not responsible for the thought. It came in the evolution of time. And so don't think that any one man is responsible for any one great event in this world. The earth is moving, the universe is working, all the laws of creation are working toward justice, toward a better humanity, toward a higher ideal, toward a time when men will be brothers the world over. (Applause). The evolution will not all be peaceful. It can't be. There will be conflict and blood shed; there will be prisons, there will be jails, but through it all this same humanity that has come onward and upward from the brute below us, onward and upward to where we are today, this same humanity will be growing in wisdom and strength and righteousness, and the good and the evil, the peace and the charity, the violence and all, will be combined to make man better and make the world juster and fairer than it has ever been before. (Loud applause).

(At the conclusion of the address of Mr. Darrow at the suggestion of a member of the audience three lusty cheers were given for the speaker).

CPSIA information can be obtained
at www.ICGtesting.com
Printed in the USA
LVOW01s0912010216
473151LV00028B/1080/P